Monday's
BALL

by Segun O. Mosuro

plasmoid9
productions

plasmoid9™
KiDs

Monday sat on the grass watching his friends play football. He longed to play with them, but he had been sidelined for playing terribly.

Unlike his friends, Monday had no ball of his own to practice with, so he couldn't get as good as them.

As he and his friends went home, they stopped by a shopkeeper's stall.

"I need a ball to practice with," Monday told his friends.

He turned to the shopkeeper. "Sir, how much are the rubber balls?"
"Two hundred and fifty naira," said the shopkeeper.

Monday gazed at a leather ball hanging in a net.
"You want the leather one?" asked the shopkeeper. *"It's the very best and costs ten times more."*

Monday left the stall looking a little glum, he paddled his canoe home.

When he arrived, Mama was loading her canoe with goods she would sell, *"How was your football game?"*

Monday bowed his head. "I didn't get to play, I'm not good enough. I need a ball of my own to practice with."

Mama gave him a hug. *"Son, I hate seeing you unhappy, but I just don't have enough money right now to buy a ball. Maybe next month, if my sales pick up, I'll get you a nice rubber ball."*

Monday clapped his hands. "Mama, you work so hard to buy what we need. If I went out and caught some fish and sold them, maybe I could buy my own ball!"

Mama stepped into her canoe. *"That's a good idea, son. I hope you catch lots of fish!"* She paddled off.

Monday paddled his canoe to the lagoon. He threw his bait ball into the water and a school of fish rushed to it.

He cast his net, but when he drew the net, there was nothing but a lowly crab in it.

He reached for the crab who pinched his finger. Monday flung his hand in pain, hurling the crab into the lagoon.

It was getting late, everyone started leaving the lagoon but Monday stayed. He cast his net and drew it, cast and drew, but caught nothing.

Frustrated, he flung his bait ball into the lagoon. SPLASH!

Suddenly, his net was tugged from beneath. He'd caught something!

It dragged his canoe around the lagoon.

CRASH! Monday, his canoe and his catch were beached.
Monday scampered to his net to see his catch.

It was a big one, a blue whale calf!

"The market women would pay loads of money for this fish! I could buy not just a rubber ball, but a leather ball!"

Then he heard the cries of another whale in the distance.

The calf got restless, it groaned and squealed, but it was when it let out a loud soul-wrenching cry that Monday understood its plight.

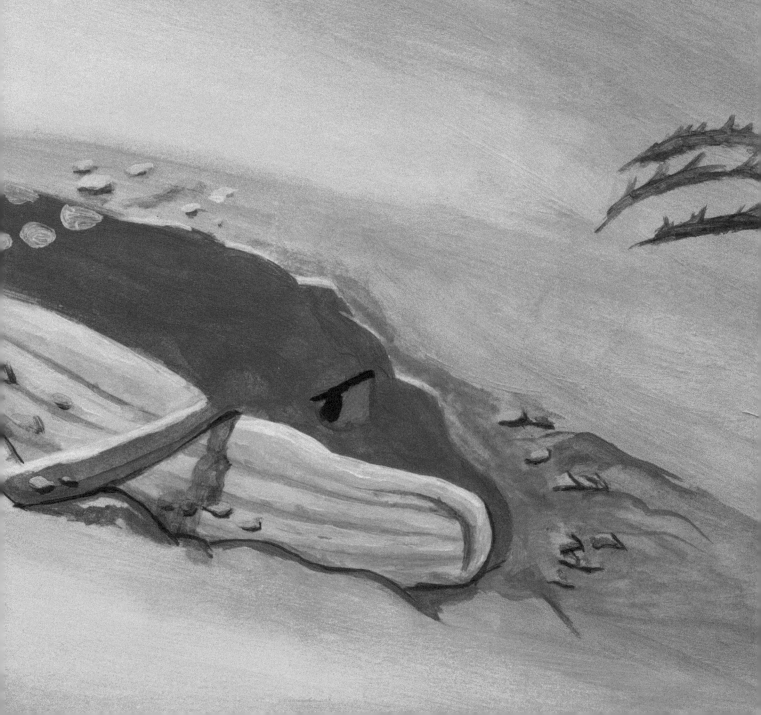

The calf had strayed from its mother.
"Should I release you? If I do, how would I buy my ball?"
Monday said to the calf.

The calf looked so sad, Monday stooped beside it.
"If I were in your fins, I'd want to be released."

With a sigh, he pushed the calf into the lagoon. He decided he'd ride out to sea and help the calf find its mother.

Storm clouds brewed in the sky, the wind howled.

Monday tied a small rope to the calf's head, powered the canoe's motor and blasted out to sea.

Mama whale's calls grew louder and louder.

When Monday saw a large fountain of water burst from the surface of the sea, he knew he had found the calf's mother.

He released the calf, who swam hastily to its mother. Their cries became a happy song, mama and baby together again.

Just then, a large wave knocked his canoe, tossing him into the sea. Monday could swim, but the waves were just too strong...

They overcame him.

The calf dove, lifted Monday and pushed him towards the shallow lagoon. Mama whale gently nudged Monday's canoe forward.

Monday woke up in his canoe, on the shore.
He was surrounded by all kinds of fish.
How did I catch them? he wondered.

In the distance, the market women were arriving in their canoes to buy fish from the fishermen.

Monday zoomed his canoe full of fish there.
The market women were so excited to see his large catch,
they bought all his fish!

"I made one hundred thousand naira!" he shouted as he ran to the shopkeeper's stall.

He bought himself a leather football and gave the rest of his money to Mama.

Monday practiced with his new ball every chance he got.

And when he finally was able to play on the field with his friends...

He scored the winning goal!

The End.

For Every Child that has a Dream - S.O.M.

Published in Nigeria in 2018 by Plasmoid9 Productions Limited
+234 908 502 0306
info@plasmoid9productions.com
www.plasmoid9productions.com

A catalogue record for this book is available from the National Library of Nigeria.

ISBN 978-978-965-563-2

Text and Illustrations copyright © 2018 Segun O. Mosuro

The right of Segun O. Mosuro to be identified as the author/illustrator of this work have been asserted.

CPSIA information can be obtained
at www.ICGtesting.com
Printed in the USA
BVHW021344241218
536329BV00004B/83/P